For my dad

temporal

troy james weaver

Disorder Press
New Orleans, LA
www.disorderpress.com

Cover Design
Peter Campanelli

Page Design
Chloe Icay

ISBN: 978-0-9975766-3-4
Library of Congress Control Number: 2017963462

I am interested in truth not facts, and I am old enough to know the difference.

—Jerzy Kosinski

Since you seldom spoke, you were rarely wrong.

—Edouard Leve, *Suicide*

A psychiatrist I once knew told me that the unconscious, that irritating retard, can't distinguish between abandoning someone and being abandoned by him. I guess he meant that even though I left you, it's come to seem as though you left me. That rings true. He also said that I was making myself into a "quiet disaster" in order to force you into returning to save me—once again a dimwit stratagem hatched by the unconscious, which doesn't recognize any of the ordinary dimensions such as time, distance, causality or your indifference.

—Edmund White, *Nocturnes for the King of Naples*

WE WERE AT a club called the Leviathan waiting for the heat from the drugs to recede. Cody overdid it, to say the least, but Samantha and I maintained our business-as-usual cool while dancing through the night. When it came to molly, we were gurus of the genre. Guess Cody snuck off to the bathroom at some point, crushed five of the fuckers up on a toilet seat and snorted them. He was out of his mind feeling good. When you have a schnozz like an aardvark and the courage to die, guess you get to feeling like Superman or something. An hour or two later he was looking pretty gross, kind of hunkered against a wall, vomit on his shoes, and we knew it was over, Clark Kent had arrived and he seemed just as weak and human as anybody else.

"What a waste," I said. "You two still owe me. Forty-five per."

"Fuck that shit," said Samantha. "Those're Shkreli prices."

"For you, thirty," I said. "But him, we'll talk about that later, you know, if he doesn't die on us."

Samantha didn't say anything, just smiled.

My phone buzzed, a text from Jared: *I think you're so beautiful. Please, please, please consider what we talked about yesterday, k? Luv u.*

I put the phone back in my pocket without a reply.

Jared was a guy from Jersey who thought I was a girl named Amber from Kansas. We were kind of dating, I guess, and I *am* from Kansas, but my real name's Aaron, and I have absolutely zero interest in fucking guys. Not saying Jared did, either, or even that there's anything wrong with that—I'm just saying he didn't know I was a guy and I did.

"Come on," said Samantha. "We could wait all night trying to get him right."

I agreed, so we hopped in my car and drove back to the suburbs, where our parents slept comfortably in their beds, snoring as if they were already dead.

We pulled into the driveway and cut the headlights. Cody fell and hit the concrete with a bang. We each grabbed an arm and hoisted him to walk.

"Ah, fuck, what the, what's that smell?" said Samantha. "Cody? You alive, man? You smell like shit."

"Shut the fuck up," he said through clenched teeth.

"Come on, guys," I said. "Not too loud."

My phone vibrated in my pocket. I thought maybe it was Jared, but that was just me being hopeful. It just as easily could have been Marcus, Marie, or Darius. It turned out to be my mom: *you coming home tonight?* I only saw this an hour later, after we got Cody covered up and hydrated and asleep. I didn't reply. Instead I texted Jared: *I know it's late, but can you talk?*

"New Order or The Smiths?" asked Samantha.

I was staring at my phone, waiting for a text to appear.

"You could at least tell me to fuck off or something," she said.

"Fuck off, then," I said.

She picked The Smiths.

I settled back in a beanbag chair, waiting. Occasionally I'd look up to see if Cody was still breathing, every now and then look at Samantha. She was pretty. She had this black hair and pale skin, and had a bit of a crooked smile, but I found it endearing. She was dancing while sitting on the floor, writhing, shaking her head—I don't know how to describe it. We were all in our own little separate worlds and those worlds were crammed into this world. It was stuffy, you know? We liked the company, yet other times we wanted those other worlds to be crushed by meteors or asteroids, just like how the dinosaurs supposedly died. It couldn't hurt much, right? Wouldn't even see it coming. You don't feel anything when you're glued to a screen, even when you're up late cooking up extinction theories.

Finally Jared texted: *I'm half sleep. Can we talk tomorrow?*

Tomorrow? Fuck tomorrow.

I typed: *it's just really...really? my bestie od'd n is in the icu and u wanna talk tomorrow?*

Jared texted: *So sorry, babe. I didn't know. I hope shes ok? she gonna make it? u holding up?*

I didn't reply.

One minute later, he texted: *hello? for real, tho, forgive me? please, baby, I didn't kno. love you.*

"Whatever, fucking asshole."

"Who're you talking to?" asked Samantha.

"Fuck you," I said to my phone as I turned it off. "Nobody, nobody, just reading some shit about the asshole we voted into office."

Samantha was still doing her amazing dances. I studied her in the mild light, and said, "You know, I think I'd rather listen to Joy Division, if you're cool with that."

"People who hang themselves after watching Herzog films probably actually aren't that rare," said Samantha.

"That's how I'd do it—right after *Fitzcarraldo*," I said, yawning.

We listened to Ian Curtis and his depressing baritone for a while, not talking to each other.

I was losing steam, finally told Samantha I was going to call it a night and go to sleep.

"Think I'll stay up for a bit longer, make sure he makes it, you know," she said. "Oh, and don't forget, we have to be on campus by eight-thirty at the absolute latest—test starts at eight-forty-five."

I nodded, slid back into the beanbag chair, covered myself with a sheet, and closed my eyes. They weren't closed all that long before I heard Cody grunt and start flopping around on the bed.

Then I heard Samantha, "You all right, Cody? You need anything?"

Then I heard him whisper, "Yeah."

"What do you need? Water?" she asked.

"Wake me up if I sleep through the fire?" he said.

"Of course," she said. "Don't worry about that."

"Thanks," he said, flopping, going back to sleep.

I finally fell asleep to his snoring, then her snoring, too, thinking stupid things, the fact of their lives lulling me into a dream where houses never burned and people never died.

WE ATE DONUTS and drank orange juice in the living room. Dad was acting weird, distant and awkward as hell. Sure it had to do with mom in some way, just couldn't say. That's just what it usually was. Had to blame someone, right? We watched *Judge Judy*, cracking jokes at the idiots suing each other for like a hundred bucks or whatever. From what Aaron told me, I guess I'd ruined the night. They weren't mad at me, though, just said I need to start taking it easy on that stuff. Overdid it like I usually do. But whatever. I was already hunting for some shrooms. Texting every dealer I knew. Plus my weed supply was running low, so why not? Might as well get whatever they had while they had it. You have to be smart about drugs, when you're looking. Never know when things will dry up.

My dad said, "Have another donut."

He was looking at Sam, biting his lower lip.

"I'm good," she said. Then she got up and said she needed to get home, had some things to take care of.

Dad followed her out into the driveway.

I asked Aaron if he thought my dad was acting funny.

"Seems just as weird as usual, man," he said.

He was busy with his phone, occasionally looking up to say something totally random.

"Can you believe koalas eat that shit?" he'd say.

"Fucking crazy what happened to Bruno," he'd say.

"Damn permafrost is melting," he'd say.

I never knew what he was talking about, just understood he had a lot on his mind and it came in spurts, disconnected.

"So, you wanna go to that party tonight?" I asked.

He didn't reply right away, then he said, "I'll leave your ass there and let the jocks rape your butt if you fuck up like you did last night."

"Yeah, I mean, it's whatever," I said.

Aaron hung out for a while, playing video games with me and my dad in the basement. Dad looked nervous or something, outside himself. Kept losing, too, like he'd never played *Mario Kart* in his life. He usually beats the shit out of both of us at those old-timey games like that, but he couldn't focus in on anything. Finally he just came out and asked me if I had any weed.

"Seriously," I said. "You don't smoke, do you?"

"Well, do you have any?" he asked.

"No, I don't," I said. "You smoke?" I laughed.

"Was just trying to see if I could trick you into telling me your secrets," he said.

Aaron laughed. "Secrets," he said. "It's no secret we smoke weed, Larry. You know that. You've caught us before."

"Yeah dad, what's going on with you? You've been acting weird all morning."

"Just don't feel well," he said. "Matter of fact, I think I'm gonna go lie down for a bit."

Aaron looked up briefly from his phone and said, "Feel better, Mister Larry."

My dad fist-bumped him and went upstairs.

WHEN HE TOLD me my house burned down I was convinced my soul went with it, a fucking burnt-out field and smoke going up and away, disappearing. Missed the final, too. We all did, but I had an excuse. I woke up to a bunch of shuffling and banging coming from upstairs. Then Cody's dad, Larry, full-on burst through the bedroom door at six in the morning, still in his briefs, yelling, "Sam, Sam, wake up! Your folks, their house is on fire."

I was shocked, *How the fuck did he know?* I looked up at Larry like what-in-the-hell-are-you-talking-about?

He said, "Get up, come on, get up, come on. What are you waiting for?!"

I laughed. "You're kidding, right?"

He looked at me with a seriousness I had never before seen in him.

"No I'm not kidding!" he said.

My chest tightened.

"Come on, I'll take you over there."

I gathered my things and followed him upstairs. He put a bathrobe on and grabbed his car keys. Cody and Aaron slept through the whole thing.

The drive over was silent. Every once in awhile Larry would reach over and touch my thigh. Creeped me out. Not saying I didn't like it, just saying it felt weird, putting into perspective, too, that we were driving toward an inferno that was supposedly my home. I know it sounds crazy fucked-up or whatever, but I hadn't even thought of my parents until I smelled the smoke. Then I burst into tears. The car stopped. Confusion reigned. Larry held me in his arms, squeezed me tight.

"It's gonna be alright. It's gonna be alright." He put his face into the top of my head, nuzzled me.

"I hope they're okay," I said.

He pulled back and said, "Oh, they're fine. They weren't there when it started. Your dad's the one who called me. Trust me, they're fine."

I brushed him off, sucked back the tears, and he started driving again.

As we got closer I could see the glittering of the firetrucks and the smoke and the flames and the streams of water. But then, when we got even closer, closer still, I realized that we weren't even in my neighborhood, that it wasn't my house on fire, just some brush in a distant field. I must have been so dazed and tired and possibly still high that I hadn't paid any attention to where we were headed.

"What the fuck, Larry? That's not my house. Just a brush fire. What is this?"

He stopped abruptly, put the car in park, and said, "Listen, shhhhh, don't be upset. This was all I could come up with. Listen, shhhhhh, I"—then he grabbed me and started kissing me, tongue all loose and in my face. I pushed him off, disgusted, wiping my mouth with my sleeve.

"What the fuck, Larry? You practically raised me. You're practically my uncle. What the fuck, man?"

He didn't fight it. He didn't do much of anything. He just started up the car and drove back to his house, no explanation, nothing.

Divorce must be a bitch.

Cody and Aaron were still passed out when we got back. It was early, but I felt dirty, so I took a long shower and went back to bed. We missed the final because somewhere in that night I'd stopped caring, about anything or anyone, including myself. We woke up at noon. Breakfast was awkward. But what could I do? I couldn't tell anybody. They wouldn't have believed me, if I told them. I could hardly even believe myself.

JARED KEPT ON texting and messaging me, even though I hadn't responded in two days. I thought if I ignored him, he'd go away, but then I got a text, said he was going to kill himself and livestream the whole thing on 4Chan, and I thought, Okay, all right, I'll fucking text him. So I told him I didn't think suicide was a good idea. In fact, I told him he was emotionally abusing me with the whole suicide shtick, and if he really loved me, like he said he did, he would cut the shit. That it was over. He just needed to accept that and move on with his life.

He didn't respond to any of it.

Two hours later I got another text: *im gonna go liv in 5min.* He even sent me a link, so I could watch it, if I wanted to.

I rushed up to my bedroom, turned on my laptop, typed the URL from the link he'd sent to my phone into Google, ENTER, and voila, there he was, rope dangling, camera rolling, some kind of country song playing. Only he didn't kill himself or anything. He'd made a doll that looked like him and hung it from his ceiling fan. In the background, off-camera, you could hear him laughing. Sounded like a dweeb, honestly, and just creepy as all fuck. I didn't want to see him die or anything, but that doll hanging there and him laughing, still alive, fucking with me, got me steaming—so fucking mad I slammed my laptop shut and texted him: *you deserve to die, you fucking asshole. abusive motherfucker. in fact i hope you do die.*

My anger was cut short by a car horn. Cody was there, waiting. We had a party to get to. I wasn't sure if it was real anger or not, anyway.

It was a jock party, filled to the brim with sexy girls and sports dudes, all the people who used to pick fights with me for liking music they thought was weird and for wearing clothes they deemed too tight and faggy. Wasn't my problem they knew nothing about fashion—the black eyes and split lips just added to the ensemble.

We were at a party with all the people who made me empathize with the school shooters of the world. Kamia Darrow was in the corner on a loveseat, sipping some pink shit from a glass and sitting on Lester Cox's football thighs, laughing. I had been in love with her for many years growing up, a huge crush of mine. Cody didn't notice what I noticed, dude never noticed anything, he was shrooming and smoking and drinking, so I knew I was on my own with this one. I even tried to point it out, that she kept looking over at me, smiling. But I didn't care, he didn't have to know what I knew. I got myself enough courage after a few minutes to actually plan a way to get over there and interrupt the conversation, maybe have a conversation of our own, but when it came time, I chickened out.

Cody was annihilated by ten. I don't really drink much but said, Fuck it, you always get to have all the fun, paid the five bucks for my red Solo cup, and filled it at the keg. I chugged it down, refilled. Chugged. Refilled. I did this five or six times before I started sipping. Had a good buzz going. Head all clogged-up in the best possible way.

Jared texted me: *Im so sorry, plz, forgiv me, you just really hurt my feelings. plz talk to me.*

I texted back: *hit me up when you're dead, asshole.*

That's when I bumped into Kamia in the hallway, spilled beer on her shirt. She smiled at me and pulled me close like she was going to kiss me or something, and whispered, "Watch where you're going, Aaron. Never know who you'll run into." Then she smiled again, a big smile, and said, "Jesus, you're drooling. Gross." She laughed. I didn't say anything. She took the beer out of my hand, chugged down half of it, and kissed me. Well, not really. She acted like she was going to kiss me then let out this humongous burp, right in my mouth, and said, "You're such a fucking nerd, Aaron." I could taste the air that lived inside her, touched her organs. I smiled and said, "Burger King. No way, I love Burger King." And we both laughed, we were laughing together, having a good time, and my phone was buzzing and buzzing and buzzing. I didn't care. What I wanted was in front of me.

Everything else was tertiary, including you.

And as you know, fun never lasts long.

Kamia and I went out back for a smoke. When we got back there, there was a huddle of dudes, bunch of noise. They were yelling at somebody. I smiled and lit a cigarette, thinking What now, you stupid fucking jocks? Then I saw it was Cody they were yelling at. He was being accused of waving his dick at some girl. Thankfully Kleeve Price, a linebacker, broke up the scene and escorted us to our car. We sat there a minute, not talking. Cody was super fucked-up, could barely even keep his head up, let alone breathe. I'd have to drive, I knew that. I know, I know, I was drunk. But trust me, it was safer that way.

THE HOLOCENE IS the period we're in? Or is it the Halcyon? The lazy period? The period of existence where barbarism and entertainment are all that matters? Most of the time they are one in the same, right? We spike our daily punch with ad after ad after ad and new reality after new reality until we are nothing more than clones drunk on bullshit. We fill ourselves up with something so empty we can never satisfy our need. Like eating air. It's the only point in human history where our lives and what we consume have become so blurred we don't really have an instrument or even a concept to gauge our realities. Philosophy has failed us. Science has failed us. Religion has failed us. We are merely hollowed holograms of previous generations. But there's got to be something in that, right? There's got to be. The way Larry kissed me the other morning, how fucked-up his whole plan had been, made me realize two things: one, I'm glad it happened; two, I want to fucking kill him. So yeah, there is something, right? This lazy, young generation I'm a part of is the most traumatized and digitized in ages, meaning I can be savage as fuck. I don't care. It's time to get moving into the next geological epoch. That, or destroy this stupid world and build it anew.

"Why you looking so long-faced, honey?" Mom was eating olives out of her martini glass.

"I'm fine," I said. "Just think I blew one of my finals."

"Is that all?"

"Yeah, mom, that's all. I'm fine," I said.

My little sister was sitting beside her, eating a Poptart.

"Can I have a sleepover tonight?" she asked.

"Well, I don't see why not."

"Cool," said Susie.

"Maybe we can get a movie at the video store."

"What's that?"

"Yeah, mom," I said. "Don't you know video stores are a dead breed?"

"Really? What about Blockbuster?"

I shook my head. "They closed like four years ago."

"Really?" she said. "I guess it has been awhile since we've rented a movie."

The last time I'd been in a video store was with Cody and his mom. We rented *Killer Klowns from Outer Space.* It was one of the first times I was allowed to be at a boy's house late. We drank soda and ate popcorn, our nerves shot and sweaty, wondering who would make the first move. But it was me. That's just the way things used to be. Cody's dad walked in on us making out. I turned bright red and stood up, but Larry just stood there a second, then said, No, no, it's okay, I'll leave you two alone. I'll get out of your hair and then you, uh, can get back to whatever it is you're doing. I was fifteen, a sophomore. Cody was sixteen. He'd been held back a year in the first grade, already had whiskers growing in and no direction in life.

When my dad got home from work, mom and Susie were in the backyard playing with our dachshund, Tabby. I was still in my seat at the dining room table, staring into my empty laptop.

Keys on the table, glass of water, a slow sigh of relief, he came over and kissed my forehead, said, "How's your day, sweetie?"

"Good," I said.

He nodded, smiling, said, "That's good," then went off to the basement to watch TV—it was just as much a part of his diet as sleeping pills.

I thought about Larry again, watching my dad walk away, about how I simultaneously wanted to fuck him and kill him, I just wasn't sure which, or both, or in what order, or why, other than knowing deep down if either or happened I'd be the one in total control of the fucking situation—how that's the only thing that can make anything great about anybody's stupid, pathetic little life.

THE NIGHT I almost keeled at the Leviathan, met a guy named Duffy. Dealer. Got his number, never really intending to use it. I already had sources. But out of nowhere everything dried-up, couldn't even find weed, so I gave him a call. He didn't answer, but immediately after hanging up I got a text message, just an address. I texted, telling him what I was after, and he texted back, but it was just the address again, nothing more. Down in the shade, several miles away from where I lived.

I pulled up to the address at about 9 PM. The house was a double-wide trailer painted gray with black trim around the doors and windows. There were toys and bikes strewn across the lot. I knocked on the front door, quietly, trying to be as discreet as possible. Finally, the door cracked open.

It was a woman, looked a bit weathered, maybe thirty-five, forty years old. Hard to tell.

"What?" she said.

"Duffy home?"

She turned around and left the door open. I went in. Duffy was sitting on a torn couch, ripping from a bong.

"What are you looking for, my dude?" he asked.

"Just an eighth," I said.

"Yeah, an eighth of what?" He took another rip.

"Just weed," I said.

"All right, sit down," he said. "Got to try this shit out."

I took a hit off the bong. It tasted good, went in smoothly and out even smoother. I didn't choke or nothing.

We sat there smoking awhile, staring at the TV, muted with the CC on, reading the words at the bottom of the screen. Drug dealers get lonely, so they try to keep their customers there as long as possible—must feel awfully used.

I had to take a leak so I asked him where the little boy's room was.

He got a look on him like *keep it down* and leaned over and whispered, "Man, not now. He's sleeping. Plus, I don't let anybody go in there when the lady's home."

My heart felt weird and slimy.

"No, I meant, I mean...where's the bathroom?" I said.

He laughed, said, "Oh, yeah, okay," then pointed.

Best thing about trailers is you can make a pretty easy escape. Unless you live in one.

I locked the bathroom door, crawled out the window, fell into some weeds and drove back home, holding back the urine, confusion blooming in bursts, not even caring I'd left the money. Or the weed. I'd just drink some vodka to get to sleep. No biggie. Good sleep's the one thing mom taught me.

TOLD CODY HIS dad was definitely acting strange. It was the day after the party. Larry just sat staring at the TV like he was a zombie or something. I also told him he was starting to worry me, too, like, *what the fuck man?*

"Are you out of you mind?" I said. "Exposing yourself to people at a party—what the fuck were you thinking?"

He sat there, silently, looking like he knew he'd done something wrong, he just didn't know how to address it. "I don't remember anything," he said. "All I remember is showing up, everything else is nothing."

"Fuck dude, seriously? I'm starting to worry about what will happen to you when I move. I don't want to have to worry about you all the time."

He didn't say anything, just nodded.

"I'm sorry," I said. "I sound like my mother."

"I know," he said. "I'm sorry I keep getting you into these situations. I know I need to slow down. Never thought I'd be one of those kids who takes their parents' divorce so hard, but, fuck it, that's me. I don't know what to do. There's nothing I can do. Maybe that's the problem. I don't know how to cope with not being in control, so I'd rather not be in control, or something. I don't know."

"I don't know, either," I said. "All I know is I'm here for you. You're my best friend. I'm not going to let you go out like that."

He nodded.

"I just, I don't know. I'm so fucking angry at everybody," he said.

I put down my phone, stood up to hug him, and said, "Stand up. Come on, man. Please just stand up."

He stood up.

Out of nowhere I felt heat in my face and I heard myself saying, "Sorry, man, but this is for your own good," then I hit him in the face, hard, like really hard, and he fell to the ground, quickly stood up, had tears in his eyes.

"What in the fuck, dude," he said, coming at me, dukes-up style.

Somehow I restrained him, got him under control, and said, "I love you, man. I just want you to know I love you."

He started bawling, came at me again. But this time he didn't swing or anything, he just hugged me, tightly, squeezed the shit out of me, and said, "I love you, too, dude. I love you, too. Thanks for being here. I need you, man. I don't want you to move. I need you. I need you. I need help, man."

"I know, I know," I said. "I'm here, man." Then, after he heaved his last few sighs under my chin, I stopped hugging him and said, "Sorry, dude— beautiful moment—but I have to take a leak."

He smiled all crooked and wet, tears still in his eyes, and said, "For sure, for sure. Go."

And so I went. I went into the bathroom and sliced at my thighs with a Lady Bic I found in the cupboard, a relic from his mother, gone for months, moved across town, divorce stuff, and didn't go back out there until I felt good enough to face the weight of our decisions, alone.

DAD WAS GETTING weirder and more distant every day. He didn't really shower anymore and just stayed around in his robe, spit-shining his anguish. Aaron and I were hanging out in the basement one day, listening to a record, and then out of nowhere all this crazy noise filled the house. We ran upstairs and my dad was in the living room recording guitar onto a four-track. I asked him what he was up to. He gave me a quick glance and quipped, "What's it look like? I'm making an album."

Aaron laughed. "You serious, Mr. Larry?"

"Do I look like I'm kidding around?"

"No," he said. "Just wondering. You were in a noise band in the nineties, right?"

Dad nodded, but didn't look up. "I made some hot dogs. You two go eat, while they're still hot."

We ate the hot dogs and listened to my dad's tinkering—noticed he was using recordings of his own diaries, distorted, reversed, and looped. I thought I heard Sam's name on the recording, but Aaron said he was pretty sure he said *slam* not Sam.

Aaron threw his paper plate away and went over to the fridge to get some grape juice, kept the door open, and said, "Jesus, when did old Larry start drinking so much. I've never seen so much booze."

I shrugged it off, said, "He's always drank—just seemed to pick up when mom left. I think it's normal. Not sure if he's going to work anymore, though."

BACK WHEN I still listened to One Direction, long before I understood that the credentials for being "cool" often start with a feeling of alienation, I thought a lot about how in the end, when people remember you, there are other things that make you who you are, what they remember, not what kind of music you were into or what kind of art you liked. Beyond that, whatever, none of it matters to anybody else, just me, and that's okay.

My pain often felt loosed to the wild, driven to connection, whatever, maybe even a communion, when I listened to sad-sap shit. Other people's pain made mine feel more bearable. It's not the easiest, being a girl in the Midwest.

I reached for a One Direction CD, put it on, and danced around while cleaning my room. I got five minutes in and realized I couldn't do it, it felt so weak and pathetic compared to other stuff.

Thing about the other music, though, is it wasn't mine alone. I only got into shoegaze because of Aaron, and I only got into the noisier weirdness because of Cody. Larry had raised him on the stuff.

I thought about listening to something else when Aaron called, asked if I wanted to go to a party with him and Cody. Usually I'd say, "I'll be ready in half an hour," but I told him I didn't feel good, which was obviously a lie. He said, "All right, cool. See you tomorrow?" I didn't say anything, just hung up. I don't know why I told him I was sick. I just wanted to lie down in my bed and listen to the rain.

FELT LIKE SAM was going through something, but she wouldn't talk about it. I tried. She wouldn't budge. Little things bothered her that had never bothered her before. I had my things too, my little secrets, so I understood not pushing her. I wanted to know, if she wanted me to know. That's how I felt about Jared, too. I would tell people, when I felt good and ready to tell them.

Jared had texted me, wanting another chance: *plz forgive me. i luv u so much. 1 more chance. i can show u im worth it.*

I put my phone down and looked at Sam. She was watching a documentary about people with elephantiasis, occasionally laughing out of sheer horror. I thought about telling her about the whole thing with Jared, then thought again, picked up my phone and bought into my own lie. I was bored with my life.

Jared, bb, of course. another chance. i've missed u. just promise me you won't do that ever again.

He texted: *omg, seriously I luv u so much. thnx for being so understanding. luv u.*

"Aaron, look at this guy. He's sitting on his own balls. Looks like a beanbag chair."

I looked up at the TV and started laughing. "Built-in luxury," I said.

Sam laughed. "You think he gets any ass?"

"With balls like that, anything's possible. Guy's like a fucking super hero."

We settled in and watched the show about the people and their enormous deformities. I admired them, just taking it as it was dealt and not complaining about it. Within an hour or so, Sam was asleep and once again I was alone. Then I got another text from Jared. It was a picture of him with his shirt off. He was a little pudgy in places but had a nice enough build. He asked me to send him a picture. I was hesitant at first, being that he thought I was a girl, but about ten minutes later I said *fuck it*, went into the bathroom and sent him a picture of my top half, completely naked. Now there were no secrets between us.

AARON AND CODY picked me up to head to the Leviathan. It was Shoegaze Night. I was pumped, we all were, so we listened to *Loveless* in the car, an album Aaron and I fell in love with the moment we heard it. His brother Joe listened to it with us the night before he robbed a gas station, got arrested, and went to prison. Aaron had an older sister, too, but she lived out of state, somewhere in Arizona, had bad taste in music. I don't know why, but Aaron was always very sweet and at the same time sinister when he talked about his siblings, as though they were funny, loving, lovable, vile, despicable strangers. His relationship with his family was just as fucked as anybody's, he just hid it better. Cody was an only child. As for me, it was just me and my little sister. *Loveless* spoke to us.

Cody cranked up the music, but I immediately turned it down, and said, "I can't believe you're moving in a month."

Aaron didn't hear me, so I said it again, louder, so he could.

"Oh, yeah," he said, "you know, gone with the wind."

"I can't believe your mom's moving, too. When's she moving?"

Aaron's dad passed away freshman year.

"She's leaving same as me, next month. I'm going off to Lawrence, she's jumping a few neighborhoods over, you know, and I'm going to have the time of my life, or try to, whatever," he said.

"You're going to be great, man," said Cody, cranking the music back up.

We stopped talking and took in the drive.

At the Leviathan, we sat in a booth, eating French fries and drinking Cokes, listening to the music, which turned out to be really bad. The DJ was horrible, mixed all the wrong songs together, played fringe shoegaze bands we didn't really like, and was a complete asshole when I made a request. Lemony hues through pink strobes of light, fog, none of it made it better. We were trying to be happy, have a good time, but I'm pretty sure I'd killed that vibe in the car when I brought up Aaron's big move to a better-than-ours, more prestigious college.

I wrapped an arm around Aaron, "I'm gonna miss you so much."

He didn't say anything, just smiled, but it was a smile that looked like it was bent up out of a frown.

Cody didn't say anything, either, just looked away, sipping his Coke.

There were no drugs that night, which was nice, really nice. It felt right that night to take it in, the shit music, my two best friends, and think about things collectively or whatever, communicate without so much as a blink of the eye. I held both their hands, squeezed them. I couldn't burden them, not yet, not there, not with all they were going through. I didn't want to tell them yet, especially because it was Cody's dad who did it, yet it was practically all I could think of. I wanted to tell them so badly I could scream.

We left an hour after we got there, found ourselves cruising the darkened streets in silence—Aaron in the backseat, face awash in cellphone light, Cody tapping the steering wheel to the beat of some Chapterhouse song, and me, I was a studied reflection in a night-tinted window, and I was doing just fine.

We ended up going back to Cody's house, so we could watch stupid movies and eat popcorn, like we had when we were a couple years younger. We started off with *Child's Play*, laughing our fucking asses off. Then we watched *Irreversible*, which was what it was. I made it to the rape scene and had to leave the room. Why doesn't watching depictions of murder have the same effect on me? Never has, either. I would rather see a woman being murdered than raped. Seems backwards, doesn't it? Or does it? Anyway, I sat out the rape scene in the bathroom. I watched the clock. After about ten minutes, I came out and it was over.

"You okay?" Cody bit down on his lip, looked worried.

"It's just that awful fucking scene," I said.

"Remember John Richmond?" asked Aaron. "That kid I had in Home Economics junior year? Goth kid?"

"Yeah, I remember him," I said.

"Yeah, he was fucked-up," said Aaron. "Well, yeah, anyways, he told me that scene made him hard."

Cody started laughing, said, "That guy had a homemade poster of Dylan Klebold in his bedroom."

"Ugh. Seriously?" I said.

"Scouts honor."

"Seriously," said Aaron, chewing popcorn.

"Well, what's next?"

They presented me with several choices, but all of them were movies I thought would make me feel bad. I needed something lighter, so we settled on *Faces of Death III*. It sounds a lot worse than it is, just a bunch of vignettes of people being murdered. But they're so funny. The unreality and low budget scares are cringe-worthy, and I mean that in the sense that they're no scarier or more realistic than a ten-dollar spookhouse run by frat boys on Halloween night. Actually, now that I'm saying it, I definitely know which is scarier—and it has nothing to do with a fucking TV screen.

"WHO IN THE fuck do you text all the time?" I just came out and said it.

"Nobody, an old friend," Aaron said. "Don't worry about it."

"Come on. I know you. You're hiding something."

"I'm not hiding shit," he said.

"Whatever, dude."

"Just mind your own fucking business, all right?" he said.

"Okay, okay, chill. No need to get all worked up."

He stood up, started pacing the room.

"Look, I'm sorry. None of my business. Forget I asked," I said.

He stopped pacing. "Are you sure? You're not going to ask me again?"

"No."

He sighed, sat down in the beanbag chair. Things were awkward and quiet a moment.

"Sorry," he said, not looking up from his phone.

I fired up the laptop and watched music videos on Youtube. Ten minutes passed before he said another word, and, honestly, I wish he hadn't.

"You ever see somebody die?"

"What?"

"Have you ever seen somebody die?"

"All the time," I said.

"No, really, have you?"

"Like, in real life?"

"Yeah, not necessarily in person, but, you know, like a real death caught on film or something?"

"Why?" I said.

"Have you, or not?"

I didn't say anything.

"Here, move, let me show you something," he said, taking the laptop.

He typed a few words into the search bar and up came a video of a guy blowing his head off with a handgun.

"I don't want to watch this, man," I said.

He shrugged and typed something else. This time it was a video of random people jumping off the Golden Gate Bridge.

"Seriously, Aaron, I don't want to watch people die. Turn it off."

Aaron looked hurt, kind of, or mad, I couldn't really tell.

"You watch stuff like this often?" I said.

"There's just something about it that's beautiful or something. I don't know, man."

"Well, for my sake," I said, "turn it off. I don't want to watch this shit."

"Fine," he said, and he played some creepy album that was like this sound collage of victims of sexual assault mixed with people screaming and noise—and it just made my skin fucking crawl.

"This is fucked," I said. "Turn it off."

"It's art, man. It's just art, okay? Nothing to worry about."

"Even art has its limits."

"Fine," he said, sighing, and shut the laptop. He walked across the room and put on a record by Big Black called *Atomizer*—grinding, loud, aggressive, offensive.

"This," I told him. "I like this. This is good."

We went up into the kitchen to get something to eat. My dad was there, looking crazy. He was smoking. Far as I knew, he'd never smoked a cigarette in his life. He didn't try to hide it, either, didn't even talk to me. He just walked out into the garage and slammed the door behind him. Said something about *That fucking bitch*, but I don't know who he was talking about.

IT WAS SUCH a relief, most of the time, and then there were other times where I'd look at myself in the mirror afterward and say *What the fuck is wrong with you?*, blood lining my thighs, making red starfish of the Band-Aids I kept in stock, plastered to my skin. Sometimes I'd burn myself, too. It was easier to hide the burns, didn't have to worry about blood on my pants.

I remember the first time, I was twelve or thirteen, and I was just trying to locate a feeling of love or care or something. My brother was a drug addict, my dad was sick, my mom worked too much, and my other siblings were long gone, in other states or married with a kid on the way. I had trouble feeling much of anything, yet I felt it all so deep inside me, locked there, and I didn't know how else to make myself feel it, the things inside me, until I unlocked it all with a razor or a flame.

I was putting Band-Aids on my thighs when Cody called to tell me he needed to borrow ten bucks.

I told him if he needed ten bucks so bad he should go and sell some plasma.

"I'm not letting any needles in, man," he said. "I have enough problems."

Sometimes, now, when I think about it, I wish he would've let the needles in.

"Fine," I said, "I've got ten. Come by, I'll roll with you. I'm bored as fuck."

"Be there in fifteen," he said.

Thirty minutes later he finally showed. I got into the car and said, "Where to?"

"Just this dude I met at the Leviathan. We're getting some good shit, my dude. Promise."

We pulled up to this ramshackle shithole and unloaded onto the lawn, knocked on the rickety door and out came this huge fat fucker with tattoos up and down the left side of his face. He had the Mountain Dew design on his left forearm, all colors faded and old, and I just kept thinking, *Fuck this, fuck this.* I had a bad feeling inside me unlike anything I'd ever felt before, at least with drug things. This was the kind of real deal drug dealer shit you see in the movies, not just some measly little score from your friends from school or work or wherever. Everything about it felt gross, including the lines of powders all lined up across the coffee table and the porno playing on the TV. I acted like I was getting a call, said, "I got to take this. I'll wait in the car."

Cody came out about a half hour later, said, "All right, we're solid."

He was already toasted, rambling on and on about how good that shit really was.

I told him to get it out, I wanted an inspection.

He dug around in his pockets, knee driving the wheel, and said, "Fuck, fuck, I left it on the fucking coffee table."

He spun a U-turn and once again we were in front of the unholy palace.

I said, "I hate this place. Something's not right with these folks."

"Ah, nah, they're okay. Stay put, I'll be right back."

He went back into it, that vortex, came back out with that primo I'd been promised, and said, "Thing about this stuff is it was a bit more expensive than originally planned. Could you throw me another twenty?"

"I ain't throwing you shit," I said. "Matter of fact, I don't even want it. You keep it—give me my fucking money back."

He tried to reason with me, but I wouldn't budge, just seemed like such a shit-show he'd been conducting from the word go, like, fuck it, who cares, it's just some damn weed. Anybody can get weed.

I WAS AT the gas station at the corner of Douglas and Seneca, just filling up the car, and out came Kamia, eating a donut. I tried to turn so she wouldn't recognize me, but didn't turn quick enough, and she came over all pretty and smug and said, "How's Aaron? Must be pretty tough being best friends with Cody, huh?"

"They're fine."

"I was just curious how he was doing, that's all. You don't have to be a bitch about it," she said.

"Yeah, okay, whatever."

"Jesus, Sam, sorry, was only trying to talk to you," she said.

"We used to be friends. Now we're not. For very obvious reasons, right?"

"Fuck you," she said, walking away, donut clenched in her fist.

I went out with Aaron after that. We went and ate some tacos then went to his house. His mom was working late, so we just smoked weed and kind of hung out. I realized I'd never checked his bookshelves. He had two large ones and they were filled with books, two rows deep, stacked on top of each other, and a bunch spread all over his room. Guess it makes sense I'd never thought to check. We usually hung out at Cody's house, especially following the divorce. Out of all of those books though, there was one that really stuck out to me, a big blue book, lying on the table beside his bed. It had some kind of military looking insignia on it. I picked it up and started flipping through it. It was like a yearbook of sorts, but filled with a bunch of pictures of guys in the military. His dad was in it, holding a python with about fifteen other guys in the jungle.

"I didn't know your dad was in the army," I said.

"Yup, he fought in Vietnam."

"Shit."

He nodded, "Yeah, he got shot and everything."

"Fuck."

"Yeah," he said.

"I'm sorry I brought it up."

"It's okay. I don't mind."

"From what I've heard he was good guy," I said. "Which is awesome—I've heard how wars can fuck you up."

"It fucked him up, too. He just didn't talk about it."

"Oh..."

"Survived a war, dies of cancer. What a fucking world we live in."

I SMOKED WEED with a homeless guy at the park downtown, broad daylight, while I was waiting for the mechanic to finish putting new brakes on my car. But something about it hit me hard, like, super fucking hard. I felt amazing, but not just weed-high, this wasn't just weed, so I asked him: *Where'd you get this? This is amazing.* And he just looked at me straight-faced and said: *Oh, that, yeah, that's not the weed, that's the meth I sprinkled in.* At first I was furious, but I kept it inside as best I could, the damage was already done. It was something I never thought I'd do, the one drug I always promised myself I'd stay away from. My brother was in prison for that shit. He crushed my family with his addictions. But then I brushed it off. It was hard not to, it felt that good, and besides, I got a whole other perspective that day. For the first time in a long time I felt like I could do anything and nothing at all and everything would be okay and nothing would matter. I thought about the party and Kamia, how Cody had ruined the whole thing. I wondered if she ever thought about fucking me. I knew the answer. The answer was no. I looked at her profile pic on Facebook, dreaming. But then I thought *I have Jared now. Who the fuck cares about that other bullshit?* I walked back across the street to get my car. They weren't finished with it. I sat there a good long while and polished the screen of my phone with spit and my T-shirt. There were smudges and dirt on it that seemed impossible to get off. I got a text right as they were telling me the car was done. I wiped away at a smudge on the counter while I paid the man with grease on his hands, nametag said Chip. The text said: *thinking about fucking Larry.* It was from Sam. I didn't reply.

I picked Cody up soon afterward and took a drive, just cruising and smoking more weed. He kept going on and on about his mom's absence. He missed her, but he kind of hated her, kept saying something about how he and his dad deserved better than that.

"Dude, your mom is an amazing mother, always has been," I said. "She gave you everything. She was the real deal. Still is. And don't play like you don't know what I'm talking about. You have a great mother. Don't take that shit for granted."

"Since when did you become so fucking preachy all the time?"

"I'm just saying, don't run around thinking that kind of shit," I said. "You're lying to yourself."

We drove on in silence for a few minutes, the trees and lines going by as quick as life seems to tick on and on until it seems nothing more than a vanishing point in a bad painting. The radio sounded like distorted foghorns. Everything burned bright across the dashboard.

"Look, it's whatever," he said. "But I was thinking, we should totally try to score some mushrooms soon. I know a guy."

"I've got twenty-five bucks I'll throw down, okay? That's it. You'll have to cover the rest."

AARON AND I watched a show about these weird-ass lepers and then another one about these dudes with huge balls, which was pretty funny. This one guy was sitting on one portion of his sack and had a plate where he kneaded dough on the other side. Like, what in the actual fuck? That's crazy, right? Poor guy. Aaron occasionally watched, but he wasn't really present, if that makes sense. He was on his phone, staring into the glare, occasionally laughing, if I made him look up for more than ten seconds at a time. Eventually he put his phone down and joined me on the futon, watched the show for a while. I pretended to fall asleep, just so I could get my head on his shoulder. Lame, I know, but I didn't know what else to do. It was nice for a few minutes. But his phone eventually buzzed and he got up, left the room for about ten minutes then came back and threw his phone next to me, still pretending, on the futon. His mom yelled for him to come downstairs and talk to her about mowing the yard or something. When he was gone, I read his texts. He was texting someone named Jared. There were pictures. He'd literally spent ten minutes taking a picture of his abs, which honestly looked pretty fucking good, like, for a guy who has never worked out a day in his life, though he looked a little strained, all red and sweaty. When he came back, I pretended like I was just waking up, and said, "Sorry, dude, my dad called. They want me to do a family thing with them—got to go."

AARON PICKED ME up while he was running errands. Then he lectured me on and on and on about how great my mom is, and I wanted to say *I know my mom is fucking great, she's my mom, but that doesn't mean that she didn't leave us,* but I didn't I say that, I didn't really say anything. I just let him rant and rant. I think he was high. Seemed like he was on something, I don't know for sure, he just didn't seem like himself. Actually, he seemed like a hyper-realistic version of himself or something. He seemed obsessed with being right, that he was saying all the right things, though that was nothing new, really.

We went downtown to the record store after scoring some shrooms and browsed the bins for a while, ran into one of the jocks who wanted to kick my ass or whatever after the party. He sneered at me when he walked in. I smiled back. Then he came up to me and said, "You're fucking crazy, aren't you? You really are. Look at you. Don't fucking smile at me, okay?"

"Landon, buddy, I've known you since we were six," I said. "You can stop it with the tough-guy routine, okay?"

"Fuck you," he said.

Aaron moved in, he knew how to navigate that kind of shit better than I did.

"Dude, back off," he said.

Aaron got right in his face and said, nearly in a whisper, "If you don't turn around and walk out that fucking door I'm going to let your little secret out. We live in a small town. Everybody will know by the end of the day, okay? Everybody. You want everybody knowing that you like any and all forms of dick?"

Landon, his face contorted, his frustration flared. "Fuck you," he said.

"It will happen," said Aaron. "If you don't leave, now, it will happen."

Without another word, Landon turned his huge ass around and walked away. Aaron had tears in his eyes.

SEEMED LIKE ALL the stupid assholes of the world were united against us. I know they weren't, but that's just the way it feels sometimes, like, *Could you please just shut the fuck up, please?* I just wanted to get home so I could sleep for a change. I was exhausted with living. But when I got home Jared texted and texted and texted until I finally gave up on sleep and started texting back.

In between a text about Jared's drug-addled dad and me telling him about my brother and how I understood certain struggles, I started getting bored, or maybe just started pulling back, I don't know, but I got Youtube up on my phone and was instantly sucked into a slew of serial killer interviews, occasionally texting back: *I feel u*, or, *I understand*, or, *im sorry*.

But the takeaway from the night was, *We are all evil, in some form or another.* And I couldn't agree more, even if it was Richard Ramirez who said it.

DON'T KNOW WHETHER I was really desperate for weed or just plain curious about that dude, Duffy, but for whatever reason, I found myself back at his trailer, on the couch, watching TV and smoking his shit. He had on *E.T.*. Every now and then he would get this weird look on his face, usually when Drew Barrymore was on the screen, and let out a weird grunt, take a sip from his Coke, repeat—didn't talk or nothing.

I saw no signs of the child or the lady from the time before.

"Where's your, uh, the lady?" I said.

He set his Coke down silently then faced me. "Why? You in the mood to fuck or something?"

I shuffled, fumbling for something to say. "No, I don't know. Why?"

"Jerry's back there now, doing his thing," said Duffy. "When he's done, you can have a go. Hundred bucks, one hour."

"No, man. I'm good. Seriously, not what I meant."

He studied me a minute. "Sure, whatever you want."

A few minutes later a man came out of the back room, sweaty, blood on his knuckles, and said, "There you go, man." He threw a hundred dollars on the coffee table. "Gets better every time," he said, and walked out, shutting the door behind him.

Whoring out his girlfriend or wife or whoever.

But fifteen minutes later, the lady, his wife or girlfriend or whatever, she came in through the front door of the trailer with a few bags of groceries. I felt a deep disgusting film take hold of me and cover my entire body, so that's when I jolted up and said, "I've got to go, man. I've got to go. Forgot about something. I'll see you later," and left.

I mean, it seems so obvious now that I should've never gone back there.

But I did, I went back, one last time, because something was eating at me from the inside, like my guts were filled with thousands of rats, yet they couldn't make a hole big enough to squeeze through, no matter how much they chewed—and even now, after I went back there, did what I did, the big blur of my life, I still feel all their grimy yellow teeth tearing into me.

I guess I'm not ready to admit I did anything wrong.

Aaron believed in the shock-value of death in videos, yet he would never understand all that fucked-up death in person. It's the kind of information you have to take your time with, process in a darkroom like a film reel, so that you can move on with things and enjoy yourself—and maybe even for the first time in your life.

AARON CALLED AND told me about Cody's behavior at the party, and, to be honest, I was stunned. Cody had always been more respectful to people than that. But we both knew he'd changed, it was undeniable. I mean that's what this is all about, isn't it?

Cody picked me up and took me out to lunch. Nothing fancy, just Taco Bell. We sat in a booth, talking about his newfangled behavior.

"Look," he said. "I'm sorry, I didn't know what I was doing."

I shook my head, said, "I know. I guess that's why it's so fucked up. You don't even remember doing anything."

"Far as I'm concerned, if I don't remember, it didn't happen."

"That's bullshit," I said. "You know that."

He shook his head, "Yeah, I know. I don't know, I'm just going through a rough patch. Things'll get better. I'm working on it."

I nodded, things went silent. We listened to people ordering their food.

Then I said, "Cody. Can I tell you something? It's a secret, and I, I don't want you to get mad at me, but I..."

He grabbed my hands, burritos between us, and said, "Shit, you can tell me anything."

I looked at him, all of him, and knew he was telling the truth, that he wouldn't judge me, if that's what you'd even call it, if I told him about his dad's sorry fucking behavior, but instead, I shook my head, and said, "No, I can't. I'll tell you, just not now. I can't. Sorry." And that was it. I was scared of everything and nothing at all, felt like I was living inside a cage inside myself inside a hole inside the earth.

That was a week before all the other shit happened, if you could believe it, I still don't, even when I'm right there, with that thick fucking glass between us, and I feel like screaming.

BEFORE MY DAD died, he told me about the one and only time he took LSD. Said it was like everything came into focus and he understood the nature of the universe, some shit like that. Anyway, I suggested we all take a day trip to Wamego, something to do together before I moved to Lawrence. Supposedly the world's supply of LSD in the early aughts was produced in a grain silo there. Only 146 miles northeast of Wichita, too. Kansas has its moments, historically and otherwise—seemed like an appropriate time to investigate them before life started. Plus, Stull isn't too far off from there, too, so why not? Supposedly the cemetery in Stull is like a gateway to hell or something, ghouls and ghosts and all that horseshit. We could go out there at night and pretend to see stuff. That's what I told Samantha. She was scared, actually believed in that kind of thing. Cody didn't care one way or the other as long as we smoked a bunch of weed beforehand.

Cody drove the whole way there, just a bunch of prairie and hills made of flint for a hundred miles or more.

We got to the silo in Wamego in the mid-afternoon, the sun scorching away the rain from the night before, making thick air out of it. We were already stoned, so we just walked around and looked at the thing from a distance. See, they had the place all fenced-off and restricted. Looked like any other silo, too, nothing special, just had a story behind it that we kind of thought was cool.

"Well," Samantha said. "That's it. Just a fucking grain silo."

"I think it's pretty cool," I offered.

"I mean," said Cody.

"Yeah, well, shit, I guess you're right," I said, pacing, feigning a smile. "What a bummer."

I spent the next hour apologizing on the way to Stull. When we got there the sun was setting, just a bleed in the sky. I'd heard from others only to drive out to the cemetery after dark, because all those shit-kicking townsfolk would follow you out there, if you weren't careful, and try scaring you off before you had the chance to meet a ghost. Fuck people. People are what the world's always apologizing for, anyway.

So we half ignored the signs and the advice and headed straight to the cemetery. Cody parked quite a ways down and cut the headlights, just to throw folks off our trail were anybody following us. But there wasn't. We were going to go out and dance on graves, commune with ghosts, see if we could find the stairway to Hell, the one we'd read and heard about all the years we were growing up.

It was dark as we raced up to the ruins of the old church, roofless and glowing in the moonlight. I have to admit, it was scary out there. Tombstones everywhere, pitch dark except for the light from our phones, and the night noises wrapped all around us like a strange blanket.

Jared sent me a picture of his dick, sticks crunched as I walked.

I shot back: *not now. ill text you when we get to the motel.*

He sent me another picture of his dick, this time both balls were in the frame, and it was captioned: *cum n get em.*

I texted: *seriously, dude, Im on a trip with my friends. can't it wait?*

"What the fuck was that?" Samantha pointed.

Cody and I looked, couldn't make anything out.

"What? Where?" asked Cody.

"Over there," Sam said, pointing through a grouping of trees.

"There isn't anything there," I said.

She looked at Cody.

"Nothing," he said, shrugging. "Don't see a thing."

We continued on, feeling our way through the plots and weeds to the roofless church, where the devil was rumored to scream at night. The only thing we heard there were our own fears amplified by silence.

WHAT A DULL way to spend our last days together. That trip was stupid, and so was the lead-up, but it was also a good gauge for how our friends fail us or something. I don't know. It was just the first time I ever felt like we were bored with being bored together. Kind of broke my heart, to be honest, but we still sure as shit tried to make the most of it.

Cody had a CD of music Larry made. Said it was his dad's new album. We listened to it on the way back to Wichita. It was just a bunch of noise with someone talking over it. Sometimes the vocal loops were straight forward. Other times they were warped and reversed. It was some fucked-up, disorienting shit—a total assault on the senses. At first we tried to laugh it off, make it fun, but after a while it became unbearable. The title written with Sharpie across the CD said: *HOUSE ON FIRE.*

"Dude, your dad is way more fucked-up than he comes off," said Aaron.

"Nah, he's not so bad."

"You don't know the half of it," I said. "This shit is crazy."

"Yeah, this is extremely unsettling," said Aaron. "Even for me, this is too much."

"All right, all right, just give it a chance," said Cody.

Aaron and I agreed to give it some time, maybe something would eventually click and we would realize the genius of Larry. However, that didn't happen. We ended up arguing with Cody over the music until I finally had had enough and just went ahead and ejected the shit and tossed it out the window onto the freeway—all that art, just a spray of confetti in the night.

When we got back to town, nobody said goodbye.

THE STUPID FUCKING fire scene with Larry was a thing from a bad film, made even worse because I couldn't get it out of my head. And the thing is I didn't care that he tried to kiss me. What mattered was the way he went about it. Fucking pig. I made up my mind a few days later, right after we got back from Stull. The only way I could get it out of me was to dig it out of him and put it back in him, paint it into his fucking skull.

I pulled a cigarette from my purse and threw it at Aaron. He didn't even notice, too busy with that stupid fucking phone.

"Earth to Aaron," I said. "Get off your phone. Talk to me."

Aaron looked up, put his phone down, "What's up?"

"Nothing, just want to talk."

"Okay, talk then," he said.

"I don't really know what to say."

"You could start with that crazy text you sent me about Larry."

"Oh, that, yeah, that's what I wanted to talk to you about," I said.

"Okay."

"I'm going to fuck him. Something happened, I can't get into it, and I just want to show him I'm really not what he thinks he wants."

"What? He wants to fuck you?"

"He came onto me a couple of weeks ago. I don't know. Maybe it's a shit plan. I don't know. God, I don't fucking know."

"Well, if that's what you want, that's what he wants, whatever, I don't really see a problem. I mean, if Cody finds out, he'll fucking flip."

"We aren't telling Cody shit," I said.

"My lips are sealed."

"Pinky promise?"

I THOUGHT I wanted to die. Then I stopped thinking about it. Then I thought I wanted to put the kid into a warmth he'd never known. But I stopped thinking about that, too. I had formulated plans for a future filled with love. I would never think again about anything, if I knew deep down that I'd never execute it into action, never—just one of many lessons I learned from my friends.

Sam was over and she was talking to me about the time Brett Buchanan came up behind her and pinched her ass. She got mad and slapped him, called him a "fucking perv" or something. He called her a bitch and walked away. Two periods later, everyone was talking about how Sam was a slut because she'd given Brett a blowjob under the bleachers, during a freshman basketball game. It wasn't true, so she said at the time, but she knew she'd never get anybody to believe her, except for the few friends she had, including me, and so the best way to fire back was to play that game herself. So she started telling everybody, "Yeah, you could hardly call it a blowjob. His penis is the size of a thimble. It's pretty impossible to do much of anything with that."

"I remember that," I said. "All of the sudden you had all the control. All the focus shifted."

"Yeah, so crazy, too, that it turned out to be somewhat true. You remember all the cheerleaders running around talking about it?"

I laughed, "Of course. You were a legend for your prophetic insight."

"That's the thing," she said. She laughed. "It was true."

"I know, I know. Brett had a tiny dick."

"No, well, yes, but no, I actually did it. I blew him," she said. "Looking back on it, I think I really just didn't want you to know. I didn't care about everybody else."

I DON'T KNOW why I didn't tell anybody. I was just intrigued. Duffy was a fucking loser, sure, but he had the best drugs in town and, with affordable rates, you can't pass that up, can you? And besides, I'd always wanted to be a detective. After some time, though, it all started weighing on me. One day it got so bad I found myself in one of the darkest tunnels of thought. I couldn't figure out anything, yet I wanted to know it all. Why? Why this and why that? I wanted to be able to know it, understand it and also be able to live with it. But I started getting this feeling like the only way to know anything was to no longer live.

Fuck this world and all that's in it. Aaron and Sam just don't understand.

Nobody understands. I can't stop with the drugs and the thoughts and the sadness, and here I am still living this empty life. Well, fuck that shit. I'm putting an end to it. Everything hurt, nothing was beautiful. Fuck you all.

Cody

I wrote it on a Starbucks receipt, while in the unfinished basement of my dad's house, holding a nylon rope I intended to hang myself with. This was the night we got back from our dumb little trip. I was listening to that song "Can't Hardly Wait", and I sat down there in the basement for a really long time, just angry and sad, but whatever, I couldn't cry, that's the thing, no matter how much I wanted to and how hard I tried, I couldn't force a single tear. Then I heard the garage door open, put the rope down and went upstairs. My dad was just walking in from the garage.

"How are you, my man?"

I started to tell him something but then I saw his glorious face burning with life and I burst into tears. He hugged me, told me it was all right to cry, then he said some shit about how he used to be a sensitive artistic-type, that he totally understands how hard this growing-up shit can be.

"It's just, everybody's leaving," I said.

"They'll be back."

"No they won't. I may be young, but I'm not fucking stupid," I said. "People don't go back to bad when they've moved on to good."

"Trust me, son. They'll be back."

You know, I thought, *you're right. I'm the one who won't be back.*

He squeezed the breath out of me. I felt like a flattened toothpaste tube. I noticed he smelled like alcohol, too. Maybe he really understood where I was. I'll give him that. Who knows, maybe he was in that same place himself.

HALO IS A shit game and everybody knows it. Cody and Sam were playing, headsets and all, just blasting away. I watched for a while, but I was bored stupid, so I started texting with Jared a bit, just shooting it, really, nothing serious, then Cody threw the controller at me and said, "For the millionth time, do you want to play?" I shook my head, didn't say anything. Ten or fifteen minutes later I looked up to see what's up with the game, but all I saw was Cody above me, saying, "Dude, what in the actual fuck? I've asked you three times if you want to go get some grub. It's like you're fucking deaf, man. Get off that shit phone, dude, and come eat with us."

So I WENT over to Cody's. I knew he wouldn't be home. Larry opened the door and let me in. He was donning a filthy bathrobe (pink, had flowers on it, smelled like shit)—looked stiff as he walked over to the love seat and sat down.

"Look," he said. "I'm really sorry. I don't know what's wrong with me. I hope you understand. I'm just not myself these days."

I didn't say anything, not at first. I just stood there looking at him. There was a bottle of gin on the coffee table, cigarette butts littered about, even on the carpet, burns here and there on the floral-print cushions.

I'd thought a lot about it, what to do, but I couldn't really do anything, so I asked him to get me a drink, gin and whatever, with ice.

He stood up, wobbled a bit, and got me a glass with ice. When he sat back down he stared at me a moment. He looked like a zombie. So this zombie just kept staring at me, then he handed me the glass and the bottle, and said, "I can't get the lid off." So I took the lid off and filled the glass, chugged down half of it.

Larry said, "Take it easy, you'll get us both in trouble."

"Maybe trouble's what I'm after," I said.

"There's no trouble. We can't have trouble. Trouble isn't an option." He burped. "Want to listen to some music or something?"

"As long as it isn't that new shit you made," I said, refilling my glass.

"Cody's not coming home tonight," he said.

"I know, you already said that."

"What's this about then?"

"I was going to fuck you," I said. "But I changed my mind."

"Listen...Sam...I said I'm sorry."

"Yeah?" I said. "Fuck you, Larry. Your apologies are shit."

He stopped trying to talk. I watched him watch TV until he fell asleep. Then I drank the rest of the bottle and drove home.

IT WAS THE day before my move. Samantha called me, she was frantic. I couldn't really get a whole lot out of her other than "Cody" and "kid" and "arrested" and I didn't really know how to calm her down, either, so I told her I'd call Larry and be over to her place in a few minutes to pick her up. But the reality is, the details were still blurry even after the call to Larry and the tear-filled chat with Sam. All we knew was Cody had been arrested for something really awful, and that he hadn't really been charged with anything yet, because they were still investigating the crime he was confessing to. He had called Larry before he turned himself in, just said, "I'm going to prison for the rest of my life. Just wanted to tell you I love you." And Larry, not fully able to comprehend this information, said, "What the fuck are you talking about, Cody?" "I put him to sleep. The kid, I sang him a song and put him to sleep," he said, and nothing, a pause, then he walked into the police station and turned himself in.

I pulled into the driveway at Sam's house and honked the horn, tapping on the wheel, impatient, waiting, and occasionally looking down at my phone to see if I had any new texts. No texts, nothing, just more waiting. I honked again.

Finally, she came out and hopped in the car.

"What the fuck is going on?"

"They're saying he killed someone," I said.

My phone buzzed. A message from Jared: *I luv u*.

I put the car in reverse and turned down the radio. Samantha was crying, but they were silent tears. She was keeping it together pretty well, considering. Something about all of this seemed so much more like a dream than reality or something. I don't know. Not really a dream, but like some kind of weird fugue or amnesia.

"Do you think he killed someone? Why would they say that? He wouldn't kill anybody, would he?" she said.

"No. Not Cody, he can't even handle the Dwyer video."

The rest of the drive was silent. When we got to Larry's, he was on the porch with a bottle of scotch in hand and a cigarette between his lips—a radical transformation from his former self.

We hopped out of the car and said hi, but he couldn't talk, was too wasted, so he just let out a bunch of burps and grunts. Sam and I each grabbed an arm, hoisted him, and delivered him to the sofa in the living room. There was an ancient tape recorder on the coffee table, a mic, and cassette tapes everywhere, weird abrasive noise coming from the stereo.

"Larry, what's going on with Cody?" I said.

He grunted, said, "He killed a boy," and slumped further down into the cushions.

"He didn't really kill anybody, did he?" said Sam.

"That's what he's said, saying he killed a boy," he said.

Sam just looked at me like what-the-fuck-now. I shrugged, said, "Guess we can go down to the police station or jail and find out what's going on."

Larry said, "No use. They're talking him still...think still...they're still talking to him."

I took the cigarette from Larry's lips and put it into my forearm. Tiny embers fell onto the carpet. I stepped on them. Sam just looked at me like I was crazy. But she didn't say anything, just kept staring, almost like she knew.

"We should just stick around here until we hear from him or something," I said.

Sam seemed to agree. Then she took the bottle from Larry and took a few big swigs, sat beside him on the sofa.

"So long as my house doesn't burn down, I'll stay as long as it takes," she said.

"So long as we figure this shit out," I said. "Guess that's the cost of living."

Larry started snoring, mouth wide, and Sam and I just sat there staring at each other.

"I think sometimes people forget how to breathe," she said. She shrugged. "Maybe that's okay. Maybe they never learned how to live in the first place, hardly even born.

TOOK ME A few weeks to hang on to the hundred bucks I needed, but as soon as I had it I went back to Duffy's place and smoked weed with him for a bit. Then I told him I wanted to give it a go, you know, with the kid. He leaned in close and said, "Hundred bucks, one hour. Anything you want."

I handed him the bill and went into the kid's bedroom. The kid was just sitting on his bed, playing with a doll. The light was dim. I sat down beside him and brushed the hair out of his eyes. He looked like a ghost just back from war, had a look in his eyes, something I imagine we'd wanted from our visit to Stull. Something I never want to see again. There was nothing in there, big eyes like drained pools. He was a shell. I put him on his back on the bed. He didn't even try to fight it. I put him on his back on his bed and slid the pillow over his face. It was stained yellow with grease. It didn't take long and he didn't fight it. When he went limp, he looked less vacant, relieved, filled with light. I crossed his arms over his chest, put his head on the pillow, made my way out the window, and drove straight to the nearest police station to turn myself in.

There were clouds. There was a sidewalk. There was a pole. There was grass. There was a flower. Then there was me. I was alive. I was so alive I looked up at the sun and knew it couldn't blind me. It peeked through dark clouds forming. And as I stood there, ready to turn it all over, I thought: *There is only us.* Then the sky boomed, gurgled, cracked itself open, and down came a weeping of rain. The clouds weren't crying for me, they were crying for all of us—cleaning the streets, making a rainbow—the loudest silence I've ever heard.

Finally I found myself working the crux of my problems onto others. Finally I shaved my legs and put on some makeup. I kept wondering what I had even meant by my plan to fuck Larry. I mean, it didn't make sense. Nothing made sense. I could just as easily have killed him, but I didn't think that would do me any good, either. Who knows? He could have been a decent person to begin with, you know? But he wasn't. Accountability can be a bitch, but that's the way it is. So I did what I could do. What else could I do? I did the only thing that could be done. I told my mom.

"Larry?" she said. "Larry fucking Daniels?"

I nodded.

"That fucking...fucking monster."

"Mom," I said. "Settle down."

"No, I'm not fucking settling down."

She snatched her purse and headed out to the garage. I followed her out there, where she surveyed the paint cans, grabbed one, and said, "Where's your father keep the brushes?"

I found one in the toolbox.

"Good, let's go," she said.

"Okay, what? Where are we going? Also, don't you need something to get the lid off?"

"Yes, thank you. Get a screwdriver," she said.

So I did. I had the brush and the screwdriver. She had the paint and the fury only mothers seem capable of conjuring. We got into the car. It was late. Mom was in her pajamas.

She parked down the street. Then she told me to keep it down and try not to be seen, as if she had done something like this before.

We crept up into Larry's driveway. Mom plopped down and pried the paint can open with the screwdriver. Then she went to work, painting. She painted and painted, splattering the driveway. When she was done we stepped back to see what she'd done. You could faintly make it out with help from the streetlight.

RAPIST in huge lettering across the garage door, black paint.

I said, "Shit, all right, let's get the hell out of here."

But she wasn't done yet. She went over to one of the flower beds in the front yard, found a pretty big rock and said, "You get a head start."

I started running.

I heard the glass from one of the windows shatter.

I was waiting in the car at this point, pulse racing, seemed too long. Then I saw a shadow stretch over the hood of the car, she jumped in, out of breath, and we peeled ass out of there.

"That'll teach that motherfucker."

And that was all she said to me. We never talked about it again. I held onto that. It was nice having a secret that wasn't mine alone. But there was still this heaviness, this emptiness—I don't know how to explain it. It was a temporary release, though, this vandalism. Shadows loom large, that's what they tell you in grade school.

I hadn't even told her yet that Cody killed a kid.

THE HOURS DRUG on and on and on, Larry snoring through most of it, and then we got the call. I dug Larry's phone out of his pocket and put it on speakerphone. It was Cody, calling from the jail. He'd been charged with second-degree murder. He'd confessed the whole thing. Investigators had done their job and decided his story panned out. Sam didn't cry like I thought she would, she just looked terrified, like truly and terrifically haunted. I didn't know what to say so I just stood there and listened. Then, after about two minutes, his time ran out, and all we could hear was a woman's voice counting down the seconds, then the drip of a dial tone. I knew that that would be last time I'd ever talk to him.

We left Larry alone to dream in his stench, couldn't find the words to even talk about it. It was weird and awful, shocking, shocked us out of even what to think. And when we had lunch the next day, the day I was supposed to move, we didn't talk about it then, either. We just talked about the stupidest shit we could think of. The world is just too heavy with all the dead people and the burning houses and the living ghosts to give such a shit all the time.

"What are you doing tonight?" I said.

"I thought I was helping you pack your shit."

"I just thought because of…"

"I'm helping you pack your shit, Aaron. Okay?"

MY MOM INTERROGATED me about being out late the night I helped Aaron move all his shit into a U-Haul.

"I got home at midnight," I said.

"No, I heard you waltz in at three AM."

"I was helping Aaron pack up the U-Haul."

"You trying to tell me it took that long? I don't buy it," she said.

"Well, whether you buy it or not, that's what happened."

She poured me some orange juice. I took it quickly, started drinking it down so I wouldn't have to talk, and walked away.

"Where are you going?"

I kept walking.

"Fine, you go ahead and go, but we're going to talk about this later," she said.

We never did.

When I got into my room, I put on *Unknown Pleasures*, sprawled out and watched cartoons on mute. I couldn't help myself. I kept thinking about the night before. About how while we were moving boxes and furniture into the U-Haul, out of nowhere I got all crazy and grabbed Aaron and kissed him. How he seemed just as surprised as I was. How he went with it. How we somehow made it all the way into the truck, onto a Barcalounger, and I was on top of him. How he undid my pants and I undid his. How it felt dangerous—we'd never done that before, not with each other. And how I knew I'd miss him more than anybody or anything I could ever even imagine having to miss. And how, right before I left, he told me he loved me. And even though I didn't say it back, I loved him too.

And now all I can think of is how he never called me back when I tried to tell him I was late—and how I'd have to have it taken care of by myself, because some secrets you don't even tell your mother. How I know there's nothing to be ashamed of, it's just what the world tells me I should feel. How

I wished he could've at least just answered one measly call, just because, because maybe he really missed me, after all, because maybe, just maybe he truly did give a shit.

But really, have you ever had to spend your afternoon at a clinic having your womb scraped out and vacuumed clean?

How about walking past people holding signs with gross, offensive imagery on them, yelling at you, full-on in your face, that you're going to hell—that you are a fucking baby killer?

How about doing it all alone?

The doctor and nurse were nice, which helped ease my anxiety as much as it could, but the feeling, the smell, the lights, all of it, was like a long drawn-out nightmare. Was like a slow-motion sickness.

And before, the things they asked—the things they had to know.

"Do you want a picture with it?"

"Footprints?"

"Is this your first one?"

"Do you want a funeral?"

And you, you all alone, vulnerable and hurting, have to tell them that you have no clue who the father is, even though he's your best friend and

he just won't answer his fucking phone.

AFTER A MONTH or so I started getting used to prison. I was rarely bored. I mostly read a ton—anything and everything. I grew to love Dostoyevsky, whatever, because he talked a lot about the condition of man and stuff. Really heavy stuff, too. It's wonderful to have companions in this shithouse, even if they're just on paper or in your head. I made my own bed. Now I make it daily. Sleep is always bad, so I talk to myself. Pretend I'm talking to my friends. Aaron and Samantha, I talk to them. I talk to my mom and dad. I even talk to the kid. We're cool. He seems much happier these days. I tell him he's just the absolute best. He knows it. He says, *Thank you.* And I say, *No, no, no. Thank you. You saved my life.*

AT THE LEVIATHAN I sipped my Diet Coke in a booth near the DJ. The molly/acid combo I'd eaten had started to take effect. There were lights flashing and shitty dance music played. The Leviathan is a lonely place, even when it's wall-to-wall packed with happy, dancing people. But I tried to make the most of it. Actually, I found some kind of new power in the fact that I was alone on a Saturday night, whole booth to myself, and how I'd have a lot of time to fill in all the empty space beside me.

But after a while I got bored, left my car there, and walked the eight miles home. On the way, at a peak moment, a tiny little squirrel started following me. Not just tailing me, but seriously like a foot or so away from my heels, so finally I stopped and asked him what on earth he meant by following a young woman like that, in the middle of the night, and he looked up at me, all pouty-faced, and said, "I'm lonely. I just want some company." He was really cute and convincing so I scooped him up into my hands, put him into my purse, and said, "Me too." It was comforting having him there. We went to the park together and just looked at things, grooved on the weird lights in the sky. Before I fell asleep, he looked at me pensively, just silent for a few minutes, and then he erupted with: *Baudrillard, you know, he'd say that your pain isn't even real, just a side effect of a delusion—the delusion being your life.*

I said something like, "Fuck you, squirrel! That's not even original. Isn't that a line from *Fight Club* or something?"

"Truth is truth no matter where you find it," he said, putting his head on my leg. "I'm super tired. Let's go to sleep."

When I woke up in the morning, I was in the sandbox at the park and there was a dead possum in my purse, blood all over my arms, my shirt, and my pants. I buried him in the sandbox and walked several miles back to my car, the sun blinding me as it rose.

I'M NOT GOING to give you all the intimate details, but I'll say that Sam came over, two days after my planned move date, and helped me pack away the little scraps of my life into a big metal box with wheels. We spent the majority of the time talking about Cody, how we couldn't fucking believe it, the fucker, he'd gone and lost his mind. We were mourning our friend, but honestly, in more ways than one we were damning him. Life sometimes feels like one big mourning for all of mankind, even when you know things can be good and kind and pretty and forever, I mean, only if you make it so, but all this shit as of late, the summer of doom, made us both feel like we were saying goodbye to everything, to each other. And we were. I was saying goodbye to myself.

I got to thinking about this book I was assigned once in school called *Things Fall Apart*. I've never read it but I disagree with that title. Things don't fall apart, they implode, fade away, become never-weres. Like having a tattoo made with invisible ink. You don't remember everything clearly, details are foggy, somewhat invented, but you sure as shit remember the pain, don't you? You remember what you felt—and no, I'm not talking about scars. This is different. But that's the reality, isn't it? You feel it, don't you? I don't know, you tell me. I don't feel a thing. Everything's a mystery.

Clouds look like broken brains spilled into the ocean. Does that make any sense? It depends, I guess. That's where I was at, too.

I haven't talked to her in months.

"You look great," I said. "Love what you did with your hair."

"Really?"

"Yeah, I'd wear you like a sweater," I said.

Samantha made an Oh-really face, then said, "I am pretty fucking warm, you know?" She sounded annoyed.

"I can imagine," I said. "But you have to trust me."

She was visiting, talking to me through the glass, silently judging me, my orange clothes, my unshaven face and shaggy hair, but I was sure as shit glad she was there, even if I'd never be able to touch her.

"It wasn't the way they said it was, I'll tell you that," I said. "They say I'm a murderer. I gave that kid his fucking life back."

"No, really, what you did, you fucking killed him. There's no life in death."

I didn't say anything, just looked down at my feet.

"It is what it is, Cody. You can't change that," she said.

Then I said, "If you see my dad, will you tell him I love him?"

"He hasn't come to see you?"

"He doesn't want anything to do with me," I said.

"Yeah," she said, "I'll tell him. And what about your mom, should I tell her?"

"No, I'll tell her next time."

"Oh, she visits?" she said.

"She comes around."

THAT FIRST MONTH at KU, I started doing daily inventories. I inventoried my thoughts, in succession, my life in shorthand. The goal being: don't forget. I had an annoying roommate named Al and he'd come in sometimes while I was working on these inventories and say stupid shit, like, "Fat chick down the hall wants to fuck me," and so I'd scribble:

Asshole Al.

It's his birthday.

Birthdays are stupid.

Dad liked orange sherbet in his Dr. Pepper on his birthday.

Asshole Al.

Chairs with broken legs.

Military funerals.

Mom.

Student protests.

Saliva.

Flags on fire.

MC5.

Age.

Disease.

Death.

Deathdays are stupid, too.

Everyday is a deathday.

And sometimes Jared would call me while I was doing this, and I'd end up writing something like:

Fag.

Love.

Spring.

Bottom.

Other times I just ignored the two of them and continued in my own way:

Can't believe he liked that band.

Shitty Nu Metal.

As I Lay Dying.

Mom is a fish.

Sam is a fish.

Larry is a fish.

Jared is a fish.

Joe is a fish.

Cody is a fish.

Dad is a fish.

I am a fish.

All of us.

We're all fucking fish.

Just waiting for the world to cut us up and throw us in a hot pan.

All ideas are stolen.

All thoughts have already been lived in.

What else is there?

Blackberries taste like shit.

Need to go grocery shopping.

Need to get some raisins.

Pop.

Pancake mix.

Fish?

Jared said the good thing is.

Don't have to tell anybody.

Mom and Dad are gone.

I don't have to tell them.

I wouldn't anyway.

I'm wrong.

Faulkner's wrong.

We aren't fish.

We're whales.

We live inside our own bellies.

I HEARD AARON's mom died from my mom, who saw her obituary in the newspaper one morning. It was a real shocker, definitely, and I felt some sadness, but I was so mad at him, too, that I went back to not caring within a minute or two. I'd been visiting Cody, I'm not sure why. I just wanted to try and understand what happened, why he did what he did—murdering a kid like he did. But soon I started realizing there's nothing there to figure out, so I stopped going to visit him. I didn't want to care for a killer. Plus, the whole thing was a big hassle most of the time. Time goes on and so will I. The paint on Larry's house will, too, apparently. I drove by one day, over a month after my mom scrawled those huge black letters across the garage door, and though the paint had slightly faded, he hadn't done anything to have it removed or painted over or anything. The window hadn't been fixed either. The drapes were blowing in the wind. I found out that a lot of moving on is not caring. I cared so much it didn't even faze me when the caring stopped, didn't even realize it. Like a movie that ends, lingers awhile in the mind—hard to remember the names of the characters, just vague recollections of plot points or movements or whatever the hell you want to call them, that's what it was like.

MY BROTHER JOE showed up late and said, "Hurry up, we don't have all day." I thought: here we are, just like everybody else, hooked through the lips and flopping for air, an invisible line forever guiding us to our inevitable deaths or something similar. He picked me up on campus by way of Kansas City, where he'd relocated after getting out of prison. I hopped into the car, slid back in the seat, and slugged his shoulder. He was sipping iced-tea, had the radio too loud, and was wiping away at smears of lipstick on his cheek. We were road-tripping to our mother's funeral in Wichita. She'd died the previous week, from pneumonia, and the news had come like a smack to the face, as my sister play-by-played her final moments to us over the speaker phone, how she'd asked for beef jerky and Coca-Cola and a crossword puzzle, how an hour before she slipped away into the nothing she felt like she was on the up-and-up, like she could run a marathon or two, which we've since concluded was a result of the steroids they were feeding her. She had only been in the hospital for two days, so there was no way to brace ourselves for it. We were told that it was acute pneumonia, nothing too serious, and she'd be out and off to a quick recovery the very day she died. She'd always been pretty healthy. Health doesn't always matter.

"How's school?"

"It's school," I said.

"Come on, Aaron. Are you going to your classes?"

"Yeah, I'm going. I've got this one professor that looks just like you—name's Professor Dickhead."

"Hey," he said. "Fuck you."

We broke into laughter.

"I'm doing fine," I said. "You don't have to worry about me. I'm the only person in our family who has ever even been inside a college building, so, like, I think I've got this."

"Shit, you're right. Good for you, brother. Good for you."

I got a text from Jared: it was a picture of him all dressed up for my mom's funeral, even though he wouldn't actually be there. He appeared to be crying. He'd captioned the picture: *thinking of you during this difficult time. Just imagine I'm with you. I am with you. All the love, Jared.*

Things flickered in the headlights and the night grew quiet.

We stopped at a gas station an hour later. Joe got a bunch of instant coffee so he wouldn't fall asleep at the wheel. Every thirty minutes or so he'd rip open a pack, take in a mouthful of crystals, and chase it down with the Coke. It must've been the recovering addict in him, like it made his heart do something beyond just pumping blood.

I gnawed quietly on a Slim Jim while Joe spewed on about the time he and a friend got fucked up from huffing gasoline. He laughed and went silent. I thought it was funny, too, this getting high on dinosaur bones, but I thought about a lot in the span of those few seconds. Crimson drinks made with bottles of gin. The way I used to look at the sun, hoping to go blind and feel my way through life. Large grain silos and drugs and all the ghosts we secretly hoped we'd never find. The piles and piles of bones in the earth and how I wished they'd never died. Wished they could pop up from the dirt and dance around in the same clothes they wore to their funerals. Mom and dad, too—I couldn't stop thinking about them. Neither one of them could dance. But they sure could sing. And then there was Sam, I couldn't take my mind off her. She flickered through between every other thought like she was some kind of poltergeist, haunting even the memories of things that happened before she was ever there at all.

"You okay, little brother?"

"Yeah," I said. "Can you stop the car? I have to call somebody."

He pulled the car off on the shoulder in the night. I could see another gas station a half-mile down the road. I stood there alone for a second in the Flint Hills, staring at my phone.

Samantha answered on the second ring.

"Hey," she said. "You okay?"

"Yeah," I said, "I just wanted to tell you I got your..."

"Shut up," she said. "Don't say it. You don't know shit. You don't know what you're even saying."

And she was right. I didn't know shit. Still don't.

"Seriously," I said. "I mean it. I miss you. I love you."

"I wish he would have smothered me with that fucking pillow."

"Listen, though, for real, I think I'm ready. I can do it. I mean, I love you more than anything in the world, that's got to count for something."

"Oh my god," she said. "You're serious, aren't you?" She took a deep breath, then another. "You know what, Aaron? I've got an idea—and it's a good one. Why don't you go fuck yourself."

The gas station was all haloed with light, like it was on fire, the warmth of the Kansas air all thick, a placebo of fever, and me just dumbly numb to it all. After a minute or two I got back into the car, a rush of cool air, relief. Joe asked who I was talking to.

"Nobody," I told him.

"You know," he said. "I know about Cody. Read it in the paper."

I didn't say anything, just nodded.

"Well," he said. "It looks like you've figured it out."

"What?"

"That there's nothing to figure out."

I got a text message from somebody, didn't read it—just rolled down the window, dropped my phone into the dying night and watched in the mirror as it bloomed into shards and battery acid in the street.

I'd spent my entire life trying to forget, even when trying to remember. I hung my head out the window, facing east, and stared directly into the rising sun—breathing in the faint smell of all that ancient dirt and scattered roadkill. I wasn't trying to forget about anybody. I was trying to forget about the world.

Troy James Weaver lives in Wichita, Kansas.

Disorder Press is a sibling owned/operated small press based somewhere in America.

www.disorderpress.com